VIGILANCE

From The Earth Series
Book 3

D.W. PATTERSON

Twenty-Third Printing – August 2026
ISBN: 9798223157977

Future Chron Publishing

Hard Science Fiction – Old School

To Sarah

VIGILANCE

CHAPTER 1

John Abel Jackson never failed to marvel at the surface of Mars outside his family's dwelling in the Candor City district. The reddish color seen from afar was not as blended close up. Rock outcroppings, wind-carved edges, colored gray, blue-gray, yellow-tinged, unlike anything he had seen in pictures or on Earth. Earth deserts, he thought, are boring compared to a Martian plain with copious scattered rocks and distant reddish mountains.

John was just over nine and one-half Martian years old; he would have been a youth of eighteen back on Earth. He was in his first year at the Mars Space Academy in nearby Bradbury City. He was tall at six feet four inches but thin, like many children who were born on Mars. But his strength was equal to any Earthling his age. He had dark brown eyes that could stare piercingly if confronted, a typical Jackson male.

John and his dad had come outside on a maintenance expedition. The new EV (Excursion Vehicle) was extremely comfortable, and the ANI (Artificial Narrow Intelligence) that drove it seemed to be a big improvement over the last model. This ANI, popularly called an Annie when used for personal tasks, unlike those in the past, learned continually from its surroundings, never making the same mistake twice.

The new spacesuits were comfortable too. They had been developed on Mars for flexibility and durability. The wearer still had to limit his time in the Martian outdoors so as not to become overexposed to the ever-present radiation, and it was best to schedule outdoor activity in the middle of the day to avoid the worst of the extreme day-night temperature change.

John and his dad had about thirty minutes left to get their work done and get back before the warmth of the day turned into the intense cold of a Martian night. Because of the thin Martian atmosphere, the transition from warm Sun to cold night was fast. His dad was working on the programming of a monitoring station while John inspected it for any mechanical problems. The robot that John called Rothmeyer was busy unloading batteries from the EV.

Suddenly, John found himself on his back with his chest hurting. He sat up slowly and looked around. The EV was several meters away from him, and there was a cloud of smoke rising above it.

Rothmeyer was off to one side in pieces; John couldn't see his dad. He arose and looked down at his suit; it was darkened across the chest area, and his ribs ached, but the suit hadn't breached. He began walking, then running towards the EV.

He arrived at the EV and began yelling for his father before he realized he hadn't switched on his mic. He switched it on and ran to the other side of the machine. There, some meters away, was his dad, face down. John ran and kneeled beside his father. Before he turned him over, John noticed his dad's back rise and fall. He was breathing. John turned his dad over and was shocked by the condition of his suit. The outer layers around the stomach were vaporized. All he saw was a thin inner layer that the nano-machinery embedded in the suit had quickly replicated. The environmental system was working to replace lost air and maintain body temperature, but it couldn't keep up with the demands placed upon it much longer. John had to get his father to Candor City as soon as possible.

John yelled through the comm-link, "Dad, Dad, can you hear me?" His father didn't respond. John immediately lifted the unconscious body, bent and draped it across his shoulder, and began running towards the nearest rock outcropping.

He placed his father against the rock, facing the setting sun. It was the best he could do for now. He plugged his Annie into his dad's suit and checked his vital signs and saw they were stable, though far from normal. He needed to contact Candor as soon as possible, but how?

John thought.

He turned toward the EV and tried to raise the onboard Annie. No answer. The onboard electronics had probably been fried in the explosion.

He thought.

The only things he had for signaling were his suit radio and his Annie. And he realized, maybe his father's Annie. He ran to his father and searched until he found the Annie. He unfolded it; apparently, it worked. Now what?

The settlement was out of range of any one signaling device. But there might be a way to reinforce the transmission capabilities of the Annies and his suit radio. If he set them all transmitting the emergency signal and then could somehow create an alignment that would sum the radio waves at a distance, like waves of water summing and subtracting, he could create a kind of phased antenna array.

He ran the calculations on his Annie. He set his father's Annie on a high point. He took his Annie and placed it at the calculated distance. He would be in the middle with his suit radio. The Annies would synchronize with John's radio and each other and auto-adjust their signal's phase without John's assistance. But he couldn't help walking back and forth a short distance as he awaited a response to his call for help.

John paced and paced. The sun was getting lower. The bad news was that his suit was doing all it could to keep him warm. The good news was that the built-in photovoltaics were still working and the power levels were holding, but that wouldn't be truc much longer.

As the darkness encroached, John began to feel chilled, dizzy, and nauseated. He knew he couldn't stay out much longer. He began walking towards the outcrop of rocks where he had placed his father. He began to stumble, soon finding himself on his knees, crawling and breathing hard. He was almost there when he blacked out.

CHAPTER 2

Mars had developed into an independent human outpost since men first set foot there in the early part of the 21st century. But it hadn't been easy. Sure, the lethal atmosphere, the unceasing rain of radiation, and the need to supply everything that made human life possible were challenges. But the greatest challenge the Mars settlers had faced was bureaucratic in the form of the aging and increasingly irrelevant United Nations.

After Mars was settled, the UN determined that any Mars colony was under the auspices of its Office for Outer Space Affairs (UNOOSA). Considerable effort was made on the part of UNOOSA to make this known to the Mars settlers. But the Mars settlers also made considerable effort to ignore everything the UN office announced.

Men had settled underground on Mars because of the protection it offered to human physiology. They had also chosen underground settlements because of their defensive advantages. The Mars settlers had no delusions that the UN would do its best to stir up obstruction and even confrontation for the colonists if it could. It wasn't long until the Mars colonists were discussing freedom from interference. When war started on Earth in the middle of the century, the colonists seized the moment to declare their independence. With such a belligerent UN, they had nothing to lose.

The UN immediately began a public relations campaign to lure the Martians into subjugation. Secretly, the UN leadership used their authority as an extra-governmental agency to offer any country or any person that would bring the Martian colonists to heel a lucrative land grant and contract for managing Mars.

No person or organization took them up on their offer, at least not in public.

Kwaya Sinchi had connections. Through one of those connections, he was in touch with the head of UNOOSA; through another, he was in touch with an underground movement of hackers and criminals. These were people who would do anything for money and who had the agility to avoid serving time for their illegal deeds. Kwaya had the money to pay, inherited from his ancestors. And like his more famous ancestor, Kwaya believed that “Mars represents the main obstacle to a stable and just world order.” The UN had planted the seed that Kwaya, with his underground connections, hoped to bring to fruition.

Kwaya welcomed the unofficial envoy from UNOOSA to his Mediterranean villa. The envoy was there secretly to discuss the latest incident on Mars.

“You are sure, Mr. Sinchi, that there can be no connection between the recent incident on Mars and the UN? After all, we haven't exactly been secretive in our wishes for the future of Mars.”

“I can assure you. The person I have engaged has complete anonymity. This is not the first large-scale political action he has taken part in. You will remember perhaps the United States and Mexico border skirmishes of a few years ago.”

The envoy nodded.

“He contributed to their instigation,” said Sinchi. “The 'Society for Open Borders' had almost convinced the American government at the time to remove border restrictions. The Mexican and South American cartels would have been greatly harmed had this occurred. They hired him and a few others, and the rest, as they say, is history.”

“Very well,” said the envoy. “And you are guaranteeing that the UN will not be connected with this Martian incident?”

“Again,” said Kwaya, a bit exasperated. “Yes, absolutely.”

Sinchi continued, “We all know that a government, any government, can only claim legitimacy if it can protect the territory it governs. I intend to show the colonists of Mars, and by extension the countries here on Earth that have shown their support for the colonists by quitting the UN and joining the Mars-backed Solar Federation, that their Federation can not protect them. This particular target was chosen because of its relations with Mars activists here on Earth. Incidents will continue until they are convinced, and I assure you no one will connect any of these incidents with the UN."

CHAPTER 3

"You're a lucky man," said Dr. Arnold.

"You mean surviving the explosion?" asked Abel Jackson. Abel was a transplant from Earth. He was shorter than his son by a few inches but had Jackson eyes. His voice was commanding when he spoke, which was rarely.

"No, that you have a son who can think on his feet."

"You're right there, Doc; John's one of a kind."

"How is he?"

"Oh, he's fine."

"It was a good thing he landed in that warm, soft sand when he collapsed, preventing any more damage to his suit."

"Well, he was lucky there; he might not have lasted the thirty minutes in the cold that it took the rescuers to arrive. But you might say he made his own luck by quick thinking."

"I agree," said Dr. Arnold. "Have you seen him today?"

"Yeah, he was in here this morning before heading to school. Telling me all about the investigation into the explosion."

"Have they determined anything?"

"Only that it wasn't a malfunction."

"What do you mean?"

"Well, it is still early in the investigation, but the data trail points to some sort of tampering with the power relays, I'm afraid."

"Oh no," said the doctor.

After the doctor had left, Abel called the settlement's only law officer. Because of his experience in the militia, Daniel Keys was unanimously elected to perform the duties of local sheriff.

"Hello Daniel," said Abel. "I was just wondering if anything might have turned up since the last time we talked."

"Hi Abel, how are you?"

"I'm fine and feeling stronger all the time."

"Good to hear. As far as the investigation is concerned, I'm afraid there isn't anything new to report. But I have called for assistance; I thought the more heads involved, the better."

"Probably true, Daniel. But be careful that they are the right heads."

"I know what you are saying, Abel. I only called those I know personally from my militia training. I believe they will be trustworthy."

"Well, I should be out of here in a few days, Daniel. I'd like to meet with you and your posse at that time."

Daniel laughed, "Okay Abel, see you then, goodbye."

"Goodbye Daniel."

Just then, John's head popped inside the door. "Hey dad," he said. "Okay to come in."

"Sure John, I'm wide awake."

"Feeling better?"

"I feel fine, son, normal anyway. I'm thinking I should be out of here by next week."

"And what does the doctor say?" asked John sternly.

"Ha! You won't catch me there; the doctor is the one who suggested it just this morning."

"That's great news, Dad."

"How was the academy?"

"It was great, and the ride there and back is amazing. You wouldn't know you're moving over a thousand kilometers an hour except when you start or stop, of course. Earth's got nothing better. And when we get this underground system between all the settlements, it will really boost the economy. I almost wish I had to take the ride every day instead of just two days a week."

"It is amazing how much has changed just in the thirty years since your grandfather Donner brought your grandmother and me to Mars," said Abel. "Though in talking to some of the old-timers here before us, I think the real boost to development was when the Republic was declared. Everyone began pulling together; they didn't wait for directions from Earth. Although from what I hear, Earth was just as messed up then as now, so not much direction was forthcoming. Anyway, now we make our own decisions."

John listened intently, nodding his head.

"That brings me to a couple of things I want to discuss with you, John. First, why do you think Rothmeyer was damaged beyond repair when we went relatively unscathed in the explosion? And where do you think we should get a replacement?"

"Well, for one thing, I think that Rothmeyer was closer to the explosion's source than we were. Also, we essentially went with the punch, so to speak, because we were lighter on our feet and somewhat protected by our suits. Rothmeyer, being much heavier and lifting those heavy batteries, was more anchored when the explosion occurred. From my inspection of the remains, I think the explosive force hit him, and he was unable to give, so he broke."

"Sounds reasonable to me."

"As far as a replacement, we could get another robot from Simmons; he probably has a refurbished model."

"That would probably be the quickest and cheapest way to go. Getting a new Annie model from Earth would take at least six months on a freighter and cost twice as much," said Abel.

"If we got a new one from Earth, I wouldn't get an Annie version, Dad; I would get one of the new Ems, the Emulated Brain version. You know, the new AIs that are patterned after a human brain? Unlike an Annie, they can train themselves on incomplete and imperfect data sets. And they can adapt their programming to optimize their training, something no Annie can do. Basically, you show them what you want them to do, much as you would show a person. And they're not much more expensive than the Annie versions; most of the extra cost is in shipping."

"Yes," said Abel. "I've read some about these new Ems. But I don't think we should take the chance on something that new; not until they are well integrated into society on Earth would I be interested in them. I've read of some adaptation problems."

“I've read the same things, Dad. But I think I could keep the Em going. It would certainly put us at the forefront of robotics here on Mars.”

“I know you could, son, but you've got a lot to do as it is. I'm not sure we could spare you from your other duties. Perhaps we should stick to the Annie version this time; maybe next time we'll get an Em.”

“You're probably right, Dad. We've got a lot to do without adding another balky piece of robotics.”

“Good, we agree.”

“Next,” Abel said. “Daniel has asked for help from Bradbury; he expects some of the men he served with in the militia to come and help with the investigation into the explosion. We know the power relays were tampered with. They were deliberately overloaded with enough current to fuse them shut. To do that, someone had to bypass the motor safety protocol. I think it had to be someone here in Candor. I want a list from you of all the people you know who could change such protocol and all the people who would have access to the systems on the EV to complete such modification, okay?”

“Okay, Dad. To think that someone we know would do such a thing is appalling.”

“Yes, it is son. It's also worrisome that they might try to do something with more impact. And we don't know what or when.”

CHAPTER 4

Evram had been a whiz kid in school. He could do anything he wanted with a piece of electronics or a computer. He hadn't needed to be taught; his teachers had lavished enough praise upon him that he came to expect it. But when he failed the psychology requirement in college, something snapped. The professor who failed him was found mindlessly talking to himself in his home. He was placed in a mental hospital. Evram had disappeared by that time.

Evram found living in Earth orbit, under a false name, to be an acceptable compromise to prison on Earth. He was pretty much able to continue his work with computers, and finding customers was just as easy. Digital money supported his living arrangements, and he didn't really care to be around people anyway.

His latest customer obviously had a lot of money. Every time Evram did another little computer job, he charged more than before. The customer didn't complain. The next job should be even more lucrative than before, and Evram would almost be ready to retire. He wasn't sure where he would retire, but it would be bigger than the little rental module he now occupied.

Evram was preparing to continue targeting the same Mars settlement as before. His benefactor, located somewhere on Earth, left it up to Evram to decide what the incidents would be. As long as it was dramatic and had the possibility of being deadly, the customer was satisfied.

For this job, Evram had contacted a subcontractor knowledgeable in Mars settlements, particularly life support systems. The link was voice-only and protected by Evram's own cryptographic algorithm; even so, the voices were disguised.

"Yes," said the subcontractor. "It's the old, too much of a good thing. Too much oxygen can lead to nausea, confusion, unconsciousness, and even death. That is why the most expensive and important system on a spacecraft or in a Mars settlement is the oxygen carbon-dioxide recycling unit."

"But there must be alarms that guard system parameters?"

asked Evram.

"Yes, certainly, I will include the many system guards that might possibly be used. Of course, if you could tell me the system model number, we could be more specific."

"I'm afraid that information is not available at this point, although it might be in the future."

"Okay, so I'll put something together that will give you the basic components that all these systems must have, and then I'll list all the possible different enhancements you might run into, including system alarms."

"Very good, send the package as soon as possible, please."

"Right," said the sub. "Good doing business with you."

Evram didn't believe he would need such a wealth of information, but since his customer hadn't placed a limit on his "expenses," he might as well get the complete package.

Evram may have been the first to use one of the new Em AIs to hack a system. But such was the largess of his customer that he could afford it. He had specially trained the Em so that it was capable of doing whatever Evram needed. In this case, the Em would respond to any blocking from the compromised network and would cover all traces of Evram's exploits.

Evram had previously broken into the computer networks on Mars using a brute force method, but the next incident would be initiated in a somewhat more elegant manner. His customer had agreed to have a relay station placed on the Martian moon Phobos. A tremendous expense, but absolutely essential to getting the job done in secret.

Evram had programmed two digital avatars to represent himself and his Em, and he would be uploading them to the relay station on Phobos. From there, the time delay to Mars would be nothing compared to working with the average one-way twenty-four-minute delay that Evram had to deal with during the first incident. With the avatars so close to the surface of Mars, they would be able to deal with any surprises in real-time. To Evram's knowledge, this would be the first time such a hack was tried, but he had every confidence he could pull it off.

As Evram thought about that first incident, he remembered how surprised he was that he had been able to use a Martian government office net, but when he thought more about it, it seemed apropos. Government IT was the slackest in the solar system. From the government office, Evram piggybacked to the private network his customer wanted targeted.

The private settlement's net proved to be a lot tougher to break. Evram was delighted. He thought it a fitting target for his skills. After days of trying, he found his way in by spoofing a government emergency warning service. Evram thought that was funny; a system supposed to protect the colonists used to break into their network.

Evram had arranged the first incident as a test run. Now, with the help of his avatars, he would arrange another incident that would be more damaging and dangerous for the colonists.

The avatars had been uploaded and were poking around in the colonists' system until they found what they were looking for. The O2/CO2 exchange unit. With the model number relayed back to Evram, he could use it and the information provided by the sub to plan the next incident.

Evram was happy, his avatars were working as expected. He cheerfully informed his customer that he would soon trigger another incident. He didn't think about the victims as people, just targets.

CHAPTER 5

Abel was out of the hospital and back home. Home was a natural cave, the front of which was a common area for the settlement. It had been sealed off with a hard plastic material impregnated with a water-gel combination which stopped high-energy particles but allowed a diffuse light to enter, especially at sunset. The high arch of the cave in the atrium gave a feeling of openness in contrast to the windowless rooms that were more common.

Several families occupied the cave with the Jackson family. It was not unusual on Mars for more than one family to share a homestead and work together to provide the food and materials to keep the settlement going. It was more like a neighborhood than a commune. Each family owned their own quarters and were paid for any work they did in the settlement. The settlement was run as a business, trading goods with other settlements. Individuals also traded their expertise with other individuals and settlements. Abel was at the head of the council that made up the limited government of the Candor settlement.

Abel sat in the fading light, reading the two lists John had prepared for him. Those with the knowledge to modify the EV protocols and those with the opportunity to do so. Abel marked three names that were on both lists. Only one he did not know. The other two he could not believe would be the type to commit such a crime.

Marta, Abel's wife, entered. She had been working in the greenhouse since the loss of Rothmeyer. Before his destruction, the robot had been given a set list of duties including the greenhouse, but families were allowed to reserve his "spare" time for their own uses, just as Abel and John had done. The robot had essentially been a shared resource.

The greenhouse, another shared resource, was set in the side of the hill. This provided a large area for sunlight, which supplemented the artificial lighting, to enter through the same plastic material that was used in the atrium. Marta and others usually worked in the early morning, taking a midday break and then working again from afternoon until dusk to cultivate the plants and repair any of the automated equipment used to keep the greenhouse running. They worked as needed.

"Hi honey," said Abel as she entered. "How was work?"

"Everything was fine, sweetheart," she said. "Some pruning, some re-potting, and that was it. What are you reading there?"

"Oh this, these are lists that John prepared; I believe I mentioned them?"

"Yes dear, you did. So, anyone stand out?"

"A couple of people I wouldn't suspect and one person I don't know."

"Their names?" asked Marta somewhat impatiently.

"Oh, Albert Dixon, Joseph Johnstone, I know; and the one I don't know, Maxim Rodrigue."

"I see what you mean. We've known Al and Joe forever; I can't imagine they would do such a thing. They would never try to harm anyone intentionally. But I'm like you, I don't know the other person at all."

"Well, I'm going to turn these names over to Daniel when he gets here tomorrow and let him do the investigating; I'm not qualified."

"You're also not healthy enough yet to go running around trying to piece together this puzzle."

She kissed him on the forehead. "You rest here, dear; I'm going to get dinner ready."

Abel was left alone to watch the deepening of the sunset. Passing from Martian pink to a deep blue.

CHAPTER 6

This was a strange mission thought Rex Stamford. First, he had been contacted surreptitiously through an acquaintance. Next, he was to take the "bus" from Bradbury to Capri settlement, almost eight-hundred kilometers distant. There he was to meet a man, Mr. Roscians, unknown to Rex to discuss a job opportunity.

Rex boarded the bus at the Bradbury terminal. The bus was a large-scale version of a Mars crawler that had room for up to fifty travelers. The seats were none to plush for what would amount to a forty-hour journey. The only "luxuries" were an on-board toilet and a snack bar provided by the bus line's attendant.

Rex was seated next to a woman who was traveling to Capri settlement to see her son. Her son was a pilot for the mining company in Capri. He flew the miners up to the sulfate mines northeast of the settlement.

"Really," said Rex. "I understand they are just getting the magnesium processing up and running. A lot of good uses for those sulfates."

"Yes," said the woman. "My son says they have the processor up and going, it shouldn't be long until they can start selling some refined products. Bath salts would be nice to have again.

"And you, Mr. Stamford, do you have business in Capri?"

"I'm going to Capri for a job interview. I'm afraid I can't say much about it yet. I really don't know much about it. Like your son I'm a rocket jockey really, although I've worked many different jobs since I've been on Mars."

"Haven't we all," said the woman. "I've done everything from babysitting to accounting. Accounting, that was my profession before I came to Mars."

"I suppose on Mars a profession is just a suggestion as far as employment goes."

They both laughed. Eventually their banter died down, and Rex found himself looking out the window.

The crawler was making its way along the side of the Valles Marineris canyon complex within a few hundred meters of the rim. Rex knew the builders tried to maintain as level a road as possible but eventually they would have to climb a little as they tunneled through the Ganges Chaos to reach the rim of the Capri Chasma and Capri. But the Ganges Chaos was still more than a day away.

By the time they emerged into the Capri Chasma area Rex and the woman had just about had all the traveling they could stand. Though the seats reclined somewhat they were uncomfortable as a bed even in the lighter gravity on Mars. They were both bleary-eyed and cranky.

"I don't think I want to ever make this trip again, not until they have the tube finished," said Rex to no one particular.

The woman next to him said, "I don't blame you Mr. Stamford. I'm only staying with my son a month and I hope it's long enough for me to recover."

"I know what you mean."

It was late afternoon when they arrived in Capri. Rex said goodbye to his seat mate and headed for his room at the Capri Interplanetary Hotel. It was a fancy sounding name for what would pass as a small motel on Earth. It was all underground but at least the room promised a hot shower.

It was the following day when Rex met with Mr. Roscians.

"Now as I understand it Mr. Stamford you are well qualified to fly a Mars style hopper rocket?"

"Yes, that's correct Mr. Roscians."

"And you also have experience with orbital rendezvous?"

What rendezvous would be contemplated using a hopper, Rex wondered.

To Roscians he replied, "Yes."

"And you even have EVA experience I believe."

"Yes."

"Good, good. Now Mr. Stamford what my client needs you to do is to establish a communications relay station on Phobos."

"With a hopper rocket!"

"A modified hopper rocket," said Roscians. "I assure you it has the capability to do the job otherwise we wouldn't be using it. The establishment of this station is crucial for my client's research."

"Okay. But I will have to review the modifications before I commit myself to such an endeavor."

"Of course, Mr. Stamford. Actually, we were hoping you would supervise the modifications. You know better than anyone what is required for such an expedition. Just rest assured that whatever you need to complete the conversion will be made available to you. Also, two years pay, as reckoned for a interplanetary pilot, will be transferred to your bank account immediately upon commencement of the mission. Until then all your expenses will be paid. But there is one thing Mr. Stamford, for you to collect your pay you must complete the mission within a Martian month, and my employer would like it be kept quiet if possible."

"If you provide the funds, you say you will Mr. Roscians, I will meet your deadline."

CHAPTER 7

Daniel Keys was getting up to speed on the possibilities involved in the incident with the EV. He was aware of Abel's list and now was listening to John explain how the EV might have been sabotaged.

“The thing is,” said John. “You wouldn't believe the skill it took to change the programming and not have it noticed. You see, you can't just put in a routine to lock the power relays on because that could be overridden by the safety check routine. So, if you really wanted to lock the power relays in the on state you would have to change the routine that is directly responsible for that and the safety routine. Then you would need to change or fool the monitor routine into believing the safety routine wasn't changed.”

“So, what you are saying John is that it would take someone with an intimate knowledge of the software and the hardware. Is that right?”

“Yes. But the intimacy with which you would have to know all three of the software routines would be overwhelming for any one person. I mean this software wasn't written by just one or two people but dozens. And it has also been submitted to the computational software Annie, which then modified it to the point that some people wouldn't recognize their own code.”

“But what about this list. The one you made that listed people with the likely expertise to accomplish such changes.”

“Well sure, the list. It's my best guess as to who might be able to do it. But it is a guess, in all honesty I don't think there is anyone I know of on Mars that could pull it off.”

“Someone had to do it,” said Daniel. “Even if they didn't have the direct expertise, they had the motive to get it done, they could have enlisted the help of an ANI, couldn't they? We know it wasn't an accident, don't we?”

“Oh yes. We can be sure it wasn't an accident for the same reason that I don't think anyone on Mars could have done it even with the help of an Annie. Remember Annies don't evolve their programming they learn from examples. And without real-world input, the simulations needed to train an Annie would be impossibly prohibitive for any single person."

But maybe one of the new Ems, thought John.

"What do you mean that it would be prohibitive for any single person?" asked Daniel confused.

"I mean, Daniel, that if you think about it, the chances of it being an accident are slim. Because the changes in all the routines would have had to occur in the proper order or at almost the same time. And the changes would have to be in such a way as to reinforce the likelihood of failure.

"I mean why would all the routines change in just the right way so that they all contributed to the failure? It is more likely that any changes would cancel each other not reinforce. I'd expect the same if it were programming bugs lurking in the code that caused the failure. The conditions that would cause all the bugs to occur and in the proper sequence and fail in the proper way are highly unlikely. So, you see it isn't likely to be an accident."

"Great John," said Daniel exasperated. "What you are telling me is that it couldn't possibly be an accident, it couldn't possibly have been coding errors, and it couldn't possibly be any one person, and it couldn't possibly be an Annie. What do you think that leaves?"

He paused. "Nothing."

John shrugged his shoulders and smiled. "I guess I'm glad I'm not you."

CHAPTER 8

Rex Stamford had worked around the clock to supervise the hopper modification. He had enlisted the help of his network of acquaintances he had worked with on both Mars and Earth. The main change to the hopper rocket was the additional fuel tanks strapped like a belt around its main rocket. The extra fuel would allow the rocket engine to burn long enough to achieve a rendezvous with the Mars moon and then provide the needed retro-burn to bring the rocket back down.

Rex had borrowed the results and necessary calculations from public documents filed by other expeditions. He had enough fuel to duplicate the orbital elements of those other expeditions and rendezvous with Phobos at some nine-thousand four-hundred kilometers altitude. He had chosen a small ridge on the trailing side of the moon as his target for placing the relay station.

Rex had contracted for an expensive, made to fit EVA suit for himself, something he could keep afterwards. Even so, at no time did Roscians balk at paying the bills and he never even requested an explanation for an expense. Because Rex was able to pay a premium for all services the hopper rocket was ready on time.

On Mars the operation of hopper rockets was so common that not much attention was paid to them. But since Roscians wanted this operation to be kept under wraps, Rex would make several hops before taking off for orbit so as to throw off any unwanted observers. One thing that was different about this hop was that Rex would have no ground crew support, something that would have dissuaded him usually except for the payday he was receiving.

Rex made one last check of his bank account to see the unusually high balance before firing the hopper's main rocket. This first hop would be a short one of a few kilometers. Several hops later he was ready to fire the long burn that would give him the over two kilometers per second velocity he would need for rendezvous. Except for a few trips to Earth's moon, Rex had never been over a hundred kilometers above the surface of Mars in a rocket. But so far everything seemed to be nominal.

The navigational ANI was right on the money; Rex was mesmerized as he approached Phobos. He had seen many photos but the clarity he had from just a few kilometers above the surface was unbelievable. Soon he would take over the controls to bring the rocket down to just a few meters above the moon's surface. If all went well the station would deploy from there with only a slight impact.

Rex busied himself taking detailed pictures of the spot he thought best to deploy the station. On the slight ridge on the trailing side of the moon, the relay station would almost always be in sight of the Martian surface.

Rex brought the rocket ship down. A specially fitted compartment in the body of the rocket just below the command section would open and drop the station to the surface when Rex was ready.

He was almost in position, intently concentrating on the moon's surface when his vision blurred.

He was taken aback. He tried to clear his eyes with the back of his glove even though he was helmeted. He looked again at the moon and saw the surface blur. He realized then that it wasn't his eyes causing the blurring, it was the moon's surface! The moon was vibrating, quaking, or something. He knew that Phobos was under stress from Martian tidal gravity, but this was the first time he or anyone else had seen such an effect. He turned on the visual recorder for confirmation of what he saw.

Rex knew that the station might not be able to right itself if he just dumped it out the hatch from this height. Maybe the quake would stop if he waited, or maybe it would last long enough for him to run out of air. He couldn't take the chance of waiting; he would have to go in closer and wait just long enough for the shaking to subside a bit.

Unlike a hop on Mars the small moon's almost non-existent gravity required the approach to be similar to a docking maneuver. Rex would use the reaction control rockets to lower the spaceship to within only a meter or so above the moon's surface. At that height even if the quake continued the station should be able to land and right itself.

He jettisoned the relay station. The station hit the surface after the short drop, righted and deployed its antenna just as the ground seemed to jump upward at the hopper. Rex reacted quickly by firing the attitude rockets. He heard a scatter-shot of rock pellets bouncing off the hopper's skin. When he had achieved a sufficient angle to the moon's surface he fired the main rocket motor. The hopper jumped into motion.

Damn, thought Rex, that was close.

He ran a systems check and found one of the reaction motors to be balky but nothing else. He felt lucky. I can handle that, he thought. Now let's get back to Mars.

The hopper rocket had been fitted with a carbon fiber shield along the bottom half to deflect some of the reentry heat. Reentry wouldn't be severe though because there wasn't that much velocity to shed. Rex oriented the rocket and fired the main motor to slow down and drop from orbit.

The hopper rocket had slowed and was almost stationary about a kilometer above the Martian surface. Rex would set it down, get his bearings and hop his way back to his launch site near Capri. He was thinking of all he could do with the lump of money in his bank account when he heard the main rocket shutdown. The hopper started dropping. He tried to restart the engine, no luck, he tried again, no luck. He was dropping faster.

He remembered the old stabilizing parasail which was a safety precaution for emergencies. He deployed it but wasn't sure it would have any effect on slowing his velocity because the height above the ground wasn't optimal. The hopper continued to drop but just before it hit the surface he felt the parasail's tug.

It was a rough landing, Rex was shaken.

When he had collected himself, Rex found he was still in one piece. But the hopper rocket was split open with the cockpit exposed to the elements, luckily his suit was intact. He scrambled to extricate himself from the wreckage.

On the ground, he opened his Annie, it still worked. The first thing he did was check his bank balance.

Anyone observing the scene would have been amazed at the animated gestures coming from the space-suited man that had just crashed a hopper rocket. But there was a reason.

The bank account was empty, or nearly, Rex now knew why he had crashed.

CHAPTER 9

Al Dixon was on his way home after having been interviewed by Daniel. It was hard to believe they were even considering him as one of the suspects. He wasn't motivated by any political or social animosity, and he certainly wouldn't do anything to hurt Abel or John.

He thought the same could be said of Joseph who went into Daniel's office after he left. He had known Joseph too long to believe he would be involved in anything so awful.

"Joseph," said Daniel. "I think we have covered most of the questions I wanted to ask you. Just one last question, why did your parents come to Mars?"

"My understanding is that there was some prejudice against their politics."

"And what were those politics?"

"The usual, small-government conservative, leaning libertarian, self-reliant type I guess."

"And do you share those beliefs?"

"Don't have to. Mars is de facto small government, and most folks are too busy trying to stay alive to have time to infringe on another person's rights. And self-reliant? If you are on Mars and don't show a good bit of self-reliance, then you won't last long. I guess that reality trumps politics every time here on Mars."

"Okay Joseph, thank you for your time and for coming in, would you ask Mr. Rodrigue to come in as you leave."

"Sure, let me know if I can help any further with the investigation. I don't like to think what the outcome could have been hadn't young John responded so well. Goodbye."

Joseph left the room and stopped to tell the man in the waiting area that he could go in. Maxim Rodrigue nodded his head and went into the office.

"Come in Mr. Rodrigue and have a seat. I'm Daniel Keys, you may call me Daniel if you wish."

"Thank you," said Maxim, "you may call me Max."

"Very well Max. I want to ask you a few questions about your job, your background and your life here on Mars, if I may."

"Of course," said Max.

"Let's begin with your job. According to my information you work as an engineer with the firm Mars Reworkers, is that right?"

"Yes."

"And what does Mars Reworkers do?"

"We design and maintain electric motors, particularly traction motors for the EV fleet."

"And what exactly do you do for Mars Reworkers?"

"I mostly write the code for motor control."

"I see," said Daniel leaning forward. "And that brings us to your background. You recently immigrated to Mars from Earth, is that right?"

"Yes sir."

"And why may I ask did you decide to immigrate?"

"I felt my future prospects on Earth were somewhat limited."

"Would you mind expanding on your answer?"

"No, I don't mind, you can easily find out about my past if you haven't already."

He paused a moment.

"I became involved in a wrongful death court case in which I was listed as one of the co-defendants just because I was an engineer on the project. The case was brought by a transit agency that charged my company with negligence in a railway accident claiming a number of lives. The case was settled out of court by my company, but I was let go. The impression in the industry was that I was at fault for the accident."

"But you were never charged with any wrong doing, is that right?"

"Yes sir," said Max. "There was never any question about the cause of the accident. It became known that the train engineer made a mistake in interpreting the locomotive's readouts. The transit authority took responsibility for the engineer's training, and the company took responsibility for a poorly designed human-machine interface. So, the settlement was mutually agreed upon. I was just collateral damage."

"Okay Max, thank you for coming in."

"Thank you sir," said Max as he rose to leave.

CHAPTER 10

"I tell you Abel this is the darndest thing I've ever heard of," said Daniel. "I don't think anyone of the three on your list had anything to do with sabotaging the EV. And I don't think anyone in Candor could do it, probably no one in Bradbury either. So, I'm stumped."

"Well," said Abel. "We are certain it wasn't accidental so therefore it had to be deliberate. Obviously, the list isn't complete. They were just suggestions, informed to be sure, but still guesswork."

"And we aren't beyond guessing yet," said Daniel.

"Are you sure none of the men you interviewed could have done such a thing?"

"I'm as sure as I can be."

"How about the new man Maxim Rodrigue?"

"You might think him the odd man out. But I checked his story, he didn't hold anything back, it happened exactly as he said it did. And since I'm sure his story is true then he has as much to lose as to gain from such a deed."

"You think so?"

"Abel, he's another immigrant coming here for a new start. How many of us aren't?"

"I know but he does have the expertise and his background is suspect even if he doesn't lie about it."

"Yeah, I know Abel. But there is something about him that says to me he was in the wrong place at the wrong time, no more. Most of us are just lucky the same hasn't happened in our lives."

"That's true. Too many people blame without realizing how close we all are to being hurt by the whims of chance. So where does that leave us?"

"That leaves us at the beginning," said Daniel. "I'm going to have to go through the longer list of suspects. Maybe we missed something that would have put one of those on the shortlist. Anyway, my help should be arriving in a couple of days. That should make going through the longer list easier."

"I suppose so. But that is going to take some time. Meanwhile any one of us could be in the way of whatever these people are after. We need motives, that's what we need."

"Yeah, motives, a suspect, an arrest, a conviction, that just about sums it up, I think," Daniel said in exasperation.

"We need one other thing Daniel."

"What's that?"

"A break."

CHAPTER 11

Marta was working in the greenhouse early morning. At first, she didn't notice the symptoms. Then it was just a slight discomfort as if her breakfast had not settled properly. Before long she found herself confused about what she was doing and what she had done. Her nausea increased.

Marta headed for the airlock between the greenhouse and the atrium area. Then the vertigo hit. She felt herself spinning and closed her eyes, but the spinning wouldn't stop. Marta abruptly sat down and began to crawl towards the lock. She still had ten feet to go when she passed out.

She awoke in the atrium on one of the lounges. Her husband Abel was there and so was Hermann Adler who worked in the greenhouse with her. "How do you feel honey?" asked Abel.

"My head hurts and the room is spinning a bit when I turn my head. What happened?"

"John is in the greenhouse right now trying to find out," said Hermann.

"What!" she exclaimed. "You let John go in there."

"Don't worry honey," said Abel. "John is suited up; he should be protected from whatever caused you to pass out."

Just then John came through the greenhouse door carrying someone across his shoulder. He moved to where Abel and Hermann were standing and they helped him place the body on another lounge.

"Lauren," Hermann said. "I didn't know anyone else was in there."

"I found her in the far corner. I was checking the oxygen concentrator panel and almost tripped over her. Maybe that was what she was trying to do when she succumbed. I have to go back in there and finish checking."

"Okay son," said Abel. "But be careful."

John was back at the oxygen concentrator's panel. The readouts looked okay, but something was strange. They were too steady; they didn't have the tell-tale jitter that showed the cycling of the concentrator. John opened the cabinet doors. Except for the power light, the unit appeared to be in bypass. He tried the reset and the system restarted. John could hear the unit cycling as he would expect.

By the time John had returned to the atrium, Lauren had been taken to the hospital. “How's Lauren?” asked John as he unsuited.

“Not too good I'm afraid,” said his dad. “She was not responding so we had her taken to the hospital, they should be able to bring her around. What did you find in there?”

“The concentrator was offline. You wouldn't know it to look at the front panel but if you opened the door it was obvious. The oxygen hadn't been scrubbed for some time, the concentration must have been pretty high. I reset it and it seemed to start working again.”

“Let's see if I can pull up the oxygen sensors.” John pulled out his Annie. “Yeah, they appear to be working, oxygen content three times higher than normal but falling.”

“What could have caused this John?” asked Abel.

“I suspect it was the same thing as the EV dad, a bit of sabotage.”

CHAPTER 12

John worked late with his Annie that night following a hunch. He went to bed with a pretty good idea of how the incidents were happening although he still didn't know who was behind them.

"All right," said Daniel Keys the next morning. "Let me get this straight. You don't think anyone on Mars is responsible for these incidents. Is that right?"

"That's right Daniel," said John. "I suspect and I have some proof of my suspicions that these incidents were caused by a distant source. How distant I'm not sure, but the network trace I did last night leads me to believe that the source is not on this planet."

"That would explain why we haven't been able to find someone with the expertise and motive. You believe someone could break into our net?"

"It would be a challenge, but it wouldn't be impossible. The moment we tie one net to another we have a possible security breach. The only way to have perfect security is not to have inter-network operation."

"That would explain how someone could have the varied expertise and the necessary resources and remain unknown to us," said Abel who had accompanied John to see the sheriff.

"As a matter of fact," said Abel. "We can't be certain if we are dealing with just a person, an entity like a non-governmental organization or maybe a government itself. If it's a person, they are rich. If it's an NGO it would have to be a clandestine, backroom operation to protect their general interests. If it's a government, well that could be provocation for conflict with the Mars Republic. We really need to find out. This has suddenly become much more than a local criminal investigation Daniel. We are going to need some planet-wide resources to find the answer."

"John," said Abel. "Work up a report on the incidents and what you have learned, you too Daniel. We will go to Bradbury to the Attorney General and present our findings. Can you both be ready by tomorrow?"

John and Daniel nodded yes.

John and Abel met Daniel at the tube station the next morning. John and Daniel were a little bleary-eyed. This was Abel's first time on the Bradbury Express, so he intended to stay awake and take in the full experience, but John and Daniel were dozing soon after leaving Candor Station.

Abel had visited Bradbury when there was no tube link. The journey then had taken two twenty-four hour days, now it would be only an hour and was the only way anyone would even consider traveling between the two settlements. The tubes were built underground where they were protected from dust and surface weather. Evacuated of even the tenuous atmosphere of Mars the tube provided an excellent right of way, straight or only slightly curving, for the speeding cars that carried passengers and freight. Each car could carry up to fifty passengers. The car carrying Abel, John and Daniel was full, the hour of travel time gave Abel a chance to think.

Politics. A power struggle over the future of Mars even after some twenty-odd years of independence. Someone or some group on Earth has never accepted the independence declaration. The Republic's foes are getting old now, maybe this was their last chance to change the power balance.

But what were they after exactly? And why was my settlement in Candor targeted? I've never been particularly political. No, there are no Jackson's on Mars that would make clear targets. But what about Earth? Uncle Ephraim and his family are still there. I wonder if he has been up to something without informing the rest of the family? Certainly, Ephraim is prone to do exactly as he wishes, whatever the consequences. I will have to get in touch with him and find out.

He got a message from Candor on his Annie. Lauren had

regained consciousness. The internal damage was extensive, but the doctors believed that the gene therapy she was receiving would correct it. She would be in the hospital for some time but should be back home eventually.

Abel stared at the message.

That was it he thought. It was too dangerous not to pursue; he would do all he could to find out who was behind Lauren's injuries. He had to, there was no guarantee that a further threat to life was not forthcoming.

Abel closed his eyes to pray.

The presentation to the Attorney General went well. He promised to refer the matter to the head of the investigative division. They would cooperate with tracing network activity into the Jackson's settlement.

After the meeting, John pointed out that it was all well and good that the government agreed to monitor the network but to trace the next intrusion meant that there would have to be a next intrusion. And who knew what the target would be this time.

Abel said, "Yes, I agree with you John, but it is good that the government is involved even if we are going to have to do most of the work. Eventually, when we find the people responsible, we will need government authority to bring them to justice."

"You're right dad. What are we going to do now?"

"Well, Daniel is going to continue to focus on the who of the matter. I want you, John, to find a way to monitor our network and discover any intrusion before it has a chance to interfere with operations. And I am going to try to find out who off world might have a reason to cause these intrusions and why."

Daniel said goodbye and headed back to Candor. Abel and John spent the day in Bradbury visiting the Academy and some of Abel's old friends that he hadn't seen for years.

They were both quiet on the ride back. John was working with his Annie, trying to find a way to monitor all the network traffic into the settlement.

Abel spent the time drafting a message to his uncle Ephraim on Earth. Trying in a non-demanding way to find out what he had been up to. Abel wouldn't be surprised if the source of their problems began with his uncle's activism.

CHAPTER 13

Evram was getting irritated. His customer was calling, and he was getting too inquisitive. He wanted to know too many details of the next incident Evram had planned.

The customer continued, "Look, the Mars Republic is putting pressure on my people; some very important people, I just need to be able to assure them that everything is under control. And to do that I need to be able to give them some of the details of the next operation."

"But when I started this job you guaranteed me that I would have complete control, without interference or consultation," said Evram.

"Circumstances have changed."

"Not for me."

"Look, this is the bottom line. Either you give me a briefing on what you are planning next so I can get it ok'd from above, or you are out of business."

"You can't threaten me."

"I am not threatening you. I am just telling you that if you find it impossible to cooperate on this new basis, then your services are no longer needed."

"That's fine. When I get paid for the planning I've already done, then I'm out."

"Paid for doing nothing?" said the customer, laughing. "You've got to be kidding."

"If you think I'm kidding then you will find out the hard way that I am not."

"Whatever. Expect no more money or contact from me." The customer terminated the call abruptly.

Evram sat there in a rage with his Annie to his ear. He

couldn't think. He couldn't move. He had never been so insulted, treated so dismissively. It would be the last time. He didn't know who his customer was, but he would find out. And if he wouldn't pay Evram cash, he would pay in other ways.

CHAPTER 14

John was in discussion with the settlement's IT manager, April Williams. "April, we believe that someone is using our network from the outside to cause the 'accidents' we've experienced. We need a way to monitor the network and catch the intruder before he can cause more problems."

"John, I have all the cyber-security countermeasures possible already implemented. If the intrusion was from outside, we can search the activity logs for verification. But whoever got in has to be really good to outsmart the software. It should have caught any intrusive activity and reported it to me not long after the intrusion."

John nodded.

"As far as catching such an intrusion in real-time, I will have to mirror the log to a computer that's running some statistical sampling software on the continuous batches it's sent. I can set up an alert when it spots a suspicious pattern of activity. But we will first have to find signs of the intruder in the logs to imprint that pattern."

"Sounds good, April, if you want, I can run the stats on the logs to find the pattern while you get the mirror ready."

"Sure, John, and thanks."

John set up a computer to run the statistical analysis on the network logs sent to him by April. He decided to begin the run on the day before and the day of the incidents. Even on one of the fastest computers in the settlement, the analysis would take hours. He hoped he had time to find a pattern in the data before the next incident.

Abel got the answer he expected from Earth. His uncle Ephraim was involved in a movement to recognize Martian independence by the UN. Ephraim confirmed that they had a lot of opposition, and a lot of it was at the higher levels of power and authority. He was sorry about any problems his activism may have caused Abel and the others. But he pointed out that no matter how much he agitated, that was not an excuse for anyone to cause the dangerous and potentially deadly incidents that Abel had witnessed. He asked that Abel keep him informed; he would do what he could on his end to discover any connections to the incidents.

John was awakened by his Annie. The analysis was complete. He looked through the resulting numbers without any recognition. He switched to a two-dimensional view of time versus network traffic and still didn't see any obvious pattern. He used the terrain view to inspect the results. The resulting topographical representation made it clear that there were four repeatable peaks in the data which couldn't be overlooked. Using the cursor, he measured the time from peak to peak and found it to be seven hours and thirty-nine minutes for all four. The trace showed that the source of the peaks seemed to lead to the office of the local representative to the Republic's Senate. The Senator's office was close enough to wirelessly connect with the Jackson's network. But the office was probably just a proxy.

The periodicity of the data peaks was the real clue. Plenty of data could be downloaded or uploaded during those peaks. And the only reason John could think that the peaks would have that particular periodicity was that they were tied to the orbit of Phobos, Mars' innermost moon. There was no other reason that he could think of for such a period, except as maybe a subterfuge. But there was a way to check that.

He called up a planetarium program on his Annie to see where the moon Phobos was at the time of the data peaks. As he expected, the moon was over the area of Candor at those times. High enough in the sky for line-of-sight communication. Someone at some time had established at least a repeating station on Phobos and used it to break into and interfere with the settlement's net.

Before he showed the results to his dad, he wanted to run more analyses to find further corroborating evidence and the identity of the perpetrator.

CHAPTER 15

Evram wasn't following "orders". As if anyone had the right to give him orders. His customer had insisted that he wouldn't pay for any more incidents unless Evram met his demands. Apparently, the political pressure was getting too intense for his customer. Evram didn't care, but he hadn't planned the next incident for nothing. He would just give his customer a free one. He would also give him more trouble on Earth than he could believe.

Evram set out to trigger the next incident on Mars. This one was as simple as it would be deadly. All he had to do was adjust the water purification system. Just as with the O2/CO2 regulator, too much of a good thing would be deadly. Evram programmed the avatars and uploaded them.

They were in the system again.

The avatars had just gained access to the target system when the avatar Av-Em spoke up. "We have a monitor alert. I am compensating, but Av-Evram, you have already triggered a source response. Recommend withdraw. I will block and parry any attempt to trace."

Av-Evram relayed the news of the intrusion failure to Evram immediately.

"Damn," said Evram out loud some twenty minutes later. "I can't believe it."

He immediately pounded out instructions to the avatars but would have to wait almost forty minutes to know the results.

Av-Evram quickly broke contact with Mars upon receiving Evram's orders. The avatar scrubbed his trace from the colonist's system all the way back through the government office. The other avatar was withdrawing with him.

"We have exited," said Av-Em. "I suggest decommissioning of the relay station also."

"Yes," said Av-Evram as he sent the information back to

Earth before initiating the scrambler that would trash the relay station software and hardware and avatars.

"Withdrawal successful, station terminated," said the message from Av-Evram.

Evram was relieved, but now that he had a moment to think, his mood changed from one of surprise and panic to anger.

It's all your fault, thought Evram. I'll get you. You'll wish you had never heard of me when I'm finished with you.

Evram began searching for his customer. He employed all his weapons, including the Em. It wouldn't be long until he knew who had hired him, and it wouldn't be long until his customer knew that he shouldn't have crossed Evram.

CHAPTER 16

John was late getting up the next morning. He found his father in the atrium with Daniel and some of the volunteer deputies from Bradbury; among them was Rex Stamford. John showed them the results of his analysis.

"I think you've found the how of the incidents," said Abel. "And I think that I've discovered the why by messaging Uncle Ephraim."

"Don't tell me," said John. "He's involved in more activism."

"Yes, our uncle, as usual, is pursuing his beliefs to both positive and negative consequences. He is involved with a group that is trying to get the UN to recognize the right of independence for the Republic."

"The cause is good," said Daniel.

"Yes, Uncle always works for good causes," said John.

"But he often doesn't think of the antagonism he will meet," said Abel. "Well, that explains the how and the why, but who?"

Daniel spoke up, "Rex here has told me something about these people. He was hired to place a relay station on Phobos for them. Rex would you care to fill them in?"

"I've already told Daniel most of what I know," said Rex. He briefly told them what he had been hired to do. He finished up, "And I can tell you one thing, these people will stop at nothing to get their way. Even murder if necessary. They tried to kill me so that I couldn't lead the authorities to them."

"Yes," said Daniel. "And because of Rex's information we now have one of them in custody. He hasn't talked yet, but we think he can tell us a lot about the who when he does talk."

"I don't know about that," said John. "But I think I know who's behind our network intrusions."

"What do you mean, son?" asked Abel.

"I don't know who will eventually be held responsible, but I think our network intrusion involved an Em."

"An Em?" asked a surprised Daniel.

"Yes. When you think about it, it makes sense. Daniel, you

remember me telling you all the expertise it would require, and the careful timing required to cause the EV accident?"

"Of course I remember; it made my head hurt."

"Well, at the time I couldn't imagine how any one person or a group of people, no matter how smart, well-educated, and trained, could pull it off. That's when I first thought about an Em, but dismissed the thought. But when I was discussing a replacement for Rothmeyer with Dad, he pointed out what an unknown quantity Ems were. That's when it occurred to me: the possible problems with Ems are unknown unknowns. In other words, no one knows or can know what an Em is capable of because of their ability to learn.

"Now ordinarily any AI such as an Em based on a human brain would have a prohibition against doing anything that might be illegal or harm someone. But if you could train an Em to disregard that prohibition, then it would literally do anything for you. I think that is what someone has done. And that is why one entity, an Em, has all the capabilities needed to cause the incidents we've witnessed."

"That's incredible," said Daniel. "And dangerous. How could they let loose such a technology?"

"It's done," said Abel. "And there is no going back, I'm afraid. John, it will be important for you to write this up in such a way as to convince people that an Em is the only explanation for what happened here."

John nodded.

"Anyway," said Abel. "I think we have enough new information that another visit to the Attorney General's office is warranted. The fact that the entry point of the intrusion is through the Senator's office might prompt the government to redouble their efforts."

Just then, John's Annie alerted, it was the intrusion alarm that April had put on the network after John had identified the suspect pattern. They all hurried to IT.

April looked up from her screen and grimaced.

"What is it, April? Did you block the intruder?" asked Abel.

"Yes sir, we blocked him, but it is the target that concerns me."

"What is the target?" asked John.

"The water system, particularly the fluoride additive."

Abel looked at his son and then at Daniel before speaking. "Well," he said. "I guess they are serious."

"What could happen?" asked Daniel.

"It depends on the amount of fluoride we would ingest. Adults would probably just be sick, although it could lead to more serious problems like heart attack. But children could be poisoned to the point of life-threatening. And we wouldn't necessarily know what was happening until it was too late. We would probably think that it was just the flu going around."

"This should get the government involved in a serious way," said one of Daniel's deputies.

CHAPTER 17

Kwaya Sinchi had to act fast; the pressure was on. Somehow, he had to neutralize the intergovernmental request from the Mars Republic. And neutralize his hacker if possible.

He called in all favors owed him. He didn't ask any of the government operatives to lie or obstruct, but just apply the usual governmental incompetence. Slow response, no response, or wrong response would work. This was what most people expected from the government, so no one would suspect a thing.

His efforts paid off. What had at one time been a high priority request by the Mars Republic for information slowly sank into the morass of government officialdom. The clerks would pass the request in an endless circle until no one remembered such a request ever being made.

Kwaya was sitting on his balcony feeling quite pleased with his efforts when his Annie announced a caller. On the line was his banker begging Kwaya's forgiveness but saying that his estate would be in foreclosure within a week unless Kwaya could come up with the multi-millions necessary to stop the proceedings. Kwaya was disturbed and confused.

Then a call from the marina saying that his eighty-foot yacht had been repossessed and that they had been unable to stop the repo company's operative. Another call informed him that his corporate jet would be held until the back payments were made up. Kwaya was now yelling into his Annie that he owed no back payments.

It wasn't long until his Annie announced another caller. Kwaya was reluctant to answer. It was his personal banker informing him that Interpol had seized all his bank accounts and that they would be inaccessible until an investigation into the source of his funding was completed. When asked how long it would take, his banker only begged his forgiveness and suggested that with the number of Kwaya's holdings it might take several months.

Kwaya let the Annie drop from his hand. He stared at the setting sun.

Evram knew he wouldn't be able to retire soon, but he also knew of one former customer whose future looked a lot bleaker than Evram's.

He monitored the chatter over the secure government networks until he was sure they had no idea who was involved in the Martian incidents. Moreover, his former customer had done a good job blocking any inquiries, at least until Evram got finished with him.

Overall, Evram was pleased with the operation. He had broken into the colonist's network twice and created the pre-planned incidents without being caught. And when the colonists did try to trap his intrusion, he was able to get out and away without leaving a trace.

Of course, he owed a lot to his new Em. It had picked up on Evram's "methodology" quickly and had no qualms about their work. But that was to be expected; after all, Evram was also a great teacher.

CHAPTER 18

Abel had just got back from Bradbury. He got everyone together for a briefing on the ongoing governmental efforts on their behalf.

As everyone was gathering in the atrium Abel motioned for John to come over.

"Yes dad?"

"John I've been thinking. We should get one of the new Em robots from Earth. We may need it in the future to counter further intrusions. Fight fire with fire so to speak. Would you choose the model you think would be most appropriate, please."

"Sure dad."

"I also want you to pick out a replacement for Rothmeyer at Simmons place. I will get the money necessary at the next council meeting."

"Okay dad."

Abel turned to the members of the settlement that had assembled and began, "As you know we have presented the Attorney General with further results of our investigation into the network intrusions and resulting incidents we've suffered. I'm afraid that after months of investigation on the part of the Attorney General's office there has been no breakthrough in finding the culprits. However, the relay station on Phobos has been seized and is being investigated for any clues as to its origin but from what I understand it was wiped before they could get to it. Also, the government has set up security requirements for all government offices and departments which should make it more difficult for future intruders.

"As most of you know our settlement was targeted because of my family's somewhat tenuous, I have to say, connection with the ongoing effort to get the UN to recognize the Republic. Apparently, the perpetrators hoped that by targeting us we would be frightened enough to abandon the Republic's government and seek security elsewhere, specifically the UN.

"I have spoken with each settlement family head individually and I want to say publicly that my family and myself appreciate your support for staying in the Republic. As one of you said, 'They won't divide us with these coercive methods, but only make us more united.' And I appreciate those sentiments.

"But here is the bottom line. We may never know who was behind the intrusion into our network, who corrupted the Em, who almost killed Lauren. Some may think it too early to say this, but I draw this disturbing conclusion. There must be quite a bit of power and influence on the other side of these incidents to prevent a criminal investigation from making progress after several month's efforts. So much so that even the power brought to bear by this planet's government was not able to bring justice in that time. Perhaps I am wrong and in time some progress will be made, I hope so.

"But until then we have got to be watchful. I'm not saying we should be anxious and overly worried. We've taken steps that I believe are adequate to prevent further incidents initiated through our network connections. But we should be watchful because whoever was responsible for initiating these network intrusions may change tactics when they find out that path is now blocked to them.

"Because of that the council and I intend to take further steps to secure our settlement which we will announce after the next council meeting. Until then each of you should take any steps you deem necessary to protect yourselves and your families.

"For now, I just want to close by saying that for myself and my family, we have no intention of changing our lives or our routines because of these attacks. As a matter of fact, John and I are already planning our next surface expedition. But I assure you we will take the time to carefully inspect the EV before departing. We will be watchful.

"And finally, I am reminded of these words which I would like to leave you with, 'the battle is not to the strong alone it is to the vigilant, the active, the brave.' Thank you."

LOOKING BACK

This was the third and last of the novelettes finished in 2016 and published at the end the year. It didn't have a genesis from a science article or a book I had read like the first two. Rather, it was the first step in the series into the Solar System and Alpha Centauri.

Many of the stories I had read about Mars (such as the trilogy by Kim Stanley Robinson) had placed most of the settlements above ground. I chose to build underground or in natural caverns because I questioned whether a material could be found in the beginning of Mars settlement that would provide enough protection from solar radiation. Now, with the recent advances in AI and its ability to help design advanced materials, it will probably be quite possible to build on the surface from the start. But even so, I'm not sure what that material might be.

At this time the Boring Company had not been founded but soon would be (January 2017). To date it has built almost one hundred miles of tunnels and Elon Musk has suggested the technology could potentially be used to build Mars settlements underground.

THANK YOU FOR READING

Continue your journey to the stars with the next book of the 11 volume ***From The Earth Series****:*

To Tend And Watch Over

Sometimes you don't know you aren't free until the state's coercive force is used against you. And then you learn you are only free to do what big brother wants.

Davide Jackson was not as adventurous as the others in his clan. He was more a stay-at-home type.

But that doesn't mean he longs any less to be free. He just has to learn the cost of freedom.

To Tend And Watch Over is set in the future (2080s) and is a story in the **From The Earth Series** which is set in the much larger **Future Chron Universe.**

See the author's website ***www.dwpatterson.com*** for availability and more.

Hard Science Fiction – Old School.

THE FUTURE CHRON UNIVERSE

My first "universe," **Future Chron**, is complete at this time. It consists of short stories, 15 novellas, 1 short novel, and 9 novels. It is generally a far futur universe.

I have been writing in this universe since the end of 2015 (the last novel wa published in 2022).

While plot and character drive the storytelling in the **Future Chron** universe (think), physics also plays an important role. However, this is not known physic but highly extrapolated future physics. (Actually, the universe starts in the nea future when technology and science is not much different from now).

But this extrapolated physics is not "just made up" but has its genesis in curren research or popular science books. This is an important point to me, although may seem to be "made up" science and technology, it has the possibility however slightly, to come true. At least, at this point to my knowledge, nothin I've written can be ruled out.

Here is the recommended reading order for the first eleven stories.

FROM THE EARTH SERIES:

The **From The Earth Series** consists of 10 novellas and one short novel. Thes are the foundational stories of the Future Chron Universe. They follow mankind's journey from Earth to the stars (or Alpha Centauri anyway).

Whatsoever You Do - 2032 - Novelette

A pandemic had long been predicted.

Now it was happening and a former graduate student, Jack Jackson, may have the key to its containment, synthetic biology.

But because in the court of public opinion synthetic biology is feared, it has been forbidden in the money conscious halls of medical research.

How many will have to die before they change their minds?

War Through The Pines - 2044 - Novelette

What starts in space may not stay in space.

Many governments today are preparing for war in space. Most people today are unaware of it.

When will it happen? How will it be conducted? What will be the effect on a young boy just coming of age?

Vigilance - 2071 - Novelette

The history of freedom repeats itself.

And the costs are always the same.

The settlers of the new Republic of Mars were in a struggle for their freedom against powerful forces that would stop at nothing. For the Martians the costs were life, property and domestic security.

But the true cost was vigilance, eternal if need be.

To Tend And Watch Over - 2081 - Novelette

Sometimes you don't know you aren't free until the state's coercive force is used against you.

And then you learn you are only free to do what big brother wants.

Davide Jackson was not as adventurous as the others in his clan. He was more a stay-at-home type. But that doesn't mean he longs any less to be free.

He just has to learn the cost of freedom.

Union - 2090 – Novelette

How far out into the Solar System would you have to run from authoritarian powers to be free?

The answer is that there is no placc safe from the powers that would try to control you.

But in numbers, in cooperation, in pledging mutual support and fidelity, freedom might be had. For a price.

And that price is resistance, body and spirit, to those that would endeavor to control.

Circle Of Retribution - 2140 - Novelette

Gardener Jackson was one of the best pilots to ever come out of Mars Space Academy.

He was a natural to fly the missions that would mine Saturn's upper atmosphere for the fusion fuel, Helium 3, that the Solar System needed.

But there was one problem, a foe he didn't even suspect would stop at nothing to prevent Gardener from succeeding, including life-threatening sabotage.

Freedom From Want - 2153 – Novelette

The promise of Artificial Intelligence is great.

But only if Artificial Intelligence fulfills our expectations.

But what about AI's expectations? Will they be different from ours? Will AI come to believe the best way to fulfill our expectations is to manage our expectations?

If so, what of freedom?

Break Up - 2165 – Novelette

The future is predictable if not knowable and the past will repeat itself, if not in all particulars.

We know that countries have crumbled in the past and it is certain to happen again in the future.

We may think this time will be different, no doubt people in the past thought the same until their world fell apart.

Kuiper Station - 2230 – Novelette

What appeared to be a simple but ambitious goal of establishing a new colony in the Kuiper Belt, a colony to service mining activities there, was more than it seemed.

One side, led by the Solar Federation and the Jackson family, was determined to break humanity out of its centuries long stagnation and push it to embrace the stars.

The other side, led by the Terran Federation, was determined to block such expansion and maintain its power.

It would be close but the stars were calling.

The Cloud - 2328 – Novelette

It was the most audacious undertaking ever conceived by man. The building of a system-spanning Starway where giant light-sails would journey on beams of laser-light to distant stars. Not only a pathway to the stars but also an abode of life, the Starway included many space habitats built to maintain its great light focusing arrays.

But there was misunderstanding along the Starway. Misunderstanding between the Starway Corporation and the settlements.

And misunderstanding always leads to disaster.

First Interstellar - 2340 - Novella

It was a mission that no one but a Jackson would consider. But Ajax wa reluctant, he had never lead such a mission, taking a lightsail powered starshi from Earth to the Centauri System using the incomplete Star Way. He though that strong leadership would be needed. He was right.

The leader would have to handle the normal amount of human drama, both pett and serious. He would also have to handle the accidents and incidents tha would occur on a years long mission. But on this mission he would have t handle something else; direct sabotage by unknown individuals and indirec sabotage as a result of the crew's boredom and dereliction of duty.

Ajax would have to grow as a leader and a person if the Starway Centaur mission was to succeed.

www.ingramcontent.com/pod-product-compliance
Lightning Source LLC
LaVergne TN
LVHW010454160826
845677LV00012B/2474

9 798223 157977